13.96

G'day, Sydney!

Written by M. C. King

Based on the series created by Michael Poryes and Rich Correll & Barry O'Brien

DISNEP PRESS

New York

Printed in the United States of America

First Edition
1 3 5 7 9 10 8 6 4 2

Library of Congress Catalog Card Number: 2008910423
ISBN 978 1-4231-1813-8

For more Disney Press fun, visit www.disneybooks.com
Visit DisneyChannel.com

Chapter One

Miley Stewart had been on long flights before. But the flight from Rome, Italy, to Sydney, Australia, was going to be her longest ever. At first, she thought she'd heard her dad wrong. "Twenty-five *huhhhhhh*?" She gasped. Her mouth hung open in shock.

"Twenty-five hours," Mr. Stewart repeated.

Miley sat back, sinking deep into the cushy leather chair as the news sank in. Twenty-five hours. That was a really long time to spend on an airplane. Even if it was a superplush private plane.

Miley wasn't just a regular teenager. She was also Hannah Montana, pop star.

As Hannah Montana, she'd had sold-out concerts, number-one hits, and met all kinds of celebrities. Miley loved performing, but she had always known that she didn't want to be a superstar all the time. She wanted to have a normal life, too. So she and her dad had come up with Hannah Montana as a way of letting her have the best of both worlds.

As Hannah, Miley wore a blond wig and pop-star clothes. The rest of the time, she was Miley Stewart, a regular teenager from Malibu, California. Only her closest family; her bodyguard, Roxy; and her best friends, Lilly and Oliver, knew the truth.

Now Miley was on a world tour as Hannah. And that meant traveling in style. Miley looked around.

The plane for Hannah Montana's summer world tour wasn't like a regular plane. There were long, buttery leather couches and comfortable armchairs. A gigantic flat-screen TV was perfect for watching videos and playing games. And, most important, the refrigerator was stocked with every snack you could ever want. The plane was what Miley's older brother, Jackson, called a "sweet ride."

Miley had to agree. Still, twenty-five hours? Miley hadn't even known flights could take that long.

"A long flight won't phase me," said Jackson with a grin that looked suspiciously like a smirk. "I came prepared." His voice had that smug older brother tone that really got under Miley's skin.

Hannah's people had announced that Jackson was the winner of a superfan contest. One of the prizes he'd "won" was to go with Hannah Montana to all of the stops on her world tour. That way he could be on the plane with her without anyone wondering why.

Jackson didn't really want anyone to think he was Hannah Montana's biggest fan. But sometimes having a famous sister was worth the embarrassment. The tour was going to be amazing. He couldn't wait to get to Australia.

Miley watched with annoyance as her brother removed a giant pile of magazines from his backpack. He let them drop onto the long mahogany table with a thud.

"You brought magazines?" Miley asked. Jackson didn't read much besides comic books and the backs of cereal boxes.

"Not just magazines," Jackson said. "Surfing magazines. I got these at the airport newsstand. Sydney, Australia, is one of the surfing capitals of the world. By the time we arrive, I'm going to know everything I need to about the surfing scene there. I can't wait to hit the waves."

"Uh, Jackson," said Miley. Now she sounded a little smug. Clearly, her brother had forgotten an important fact: July might mean summer in Malibu and in Rome, their previous stop. But in Australia, July meant winter.

Winter as in *brrrrr*. Winter as in cold and windy. Winter as in no surfing—no way, no how!

Miley was about to oh-so-kindly remind Jackson of this when the flight attendant appeared. "Miss Montana," he said cordially, "if you wouldn't mind buckling your seat belt, we'll be taking off for Hong Kong shortly."

Hong Kong? Had Miley heard correctly? Had they gotten on the wrong plane? She could have sworn this one had HANNAH MONTANA WORLD TOUR in shimmering purple-and-gold script along the side.

"Dad, I think something's up with my

hearing," a worried Miley whispered to Mr. Stewart, "because I think he just said we're going to Hong Kong."

Robby Ray Stewart looked up from his book, *Guide to Australia,* and smiled kindly at his daughter. He had on a hat and fake mustache, part of his disguise as Hannah's manager. "That's just the first leg of the trip, bud," he explained. "We're making a quick pit stop in Hong Kong to stretch our legs and grab a bite. I've got a hankering for some egg rolls. How about you?"

"I'd take an egg roll," Jackson volunteered.

He always has food on the brain, thought Miley. It's a wonder he's not eighteen gazillion pounds.

"Count me out," groaned Roxy, rubbing her stomach unhappily. As Hannah Montana's security guard, she went everywhere Miley went. In Rome, Roxy had made it her mission to eat as much Italian ice cream as possible. Now her stomach was paying the price.

Unlike everyone else, Miley couldn't think about food right now. Because all of a sudden, an overwhelming feeling overtook her. Her eyelids started to droop. Her shoulders felt like there were bricks on top of them. And *ooh*, her feet sure ached. Miley really had walked a lot in Rome. As her aunt Dolly would say, those cobblestones were rough on the tootsies.

Miley took off her sneakers and sunk her feet into the plane's thick carpet. It felt soft beneath her socks. She zipped up the lucky Malibu hoodie that she saved for traveling. It was supersoft and cozy from being washed so many times. She propped her head on a goose-feather pillow and pulled a cashmere blanket up to her chin. For some reason, even private jets were cold.

It was weird to be so tired. After all, it was

7

only ten in the morning. Then again, touring the world, making new friends, and performing to sold-out crowds could take its toll on a girl. Even if she was having the time of her life.

Miley buckled her seat belt. She yawned, thinking of all the adventures she'd had in Rome, and the ones she'd have in Sydney. By the time the plane left the runway, she was fast asleep.

When she woke up, sixteen hours later, Jackson was right next to her. "Yo, Rip Van Montana," he shouted, cupping his hands around his mouth to make his voice louder. "Glad you finally heard me. It's time to wake up. We're in Hong Kong, and you know what that means—time for an egg roll!"

Chapter Two

For Miley, the hardest thing about being on a world tour was being separated from her best friends. So as soon as she got off the plane at the Hong Kong airport, she checked her phone for messages from Lilly and Oliver.

Her in-box was overflowing! Miley scanned the list of subject lines: OLIVER'S SOOO LAME; YOU WILL NOT BELIEVE LILLY; OLIVER THE IRRITATING. Uh-oh! It didn't seem like things were going so well back home in Malibu. It looked like her friends were sick of each other!

Oliver sent a text that said Lilly was annoying.

Lilly sent an e-mail that said Oliver was getting on her last nerve.

Oliver e-mailed that Lilly cheated in beach volleyball.

Lilly texted that Oliver couldn't hit the ball over the net. She even attached a picture of a red-faced Oliver sitting dazed in the sand. Miley cringed. Poor Oliver. A jock he was not.

Miley had only a half hour in the Hong Kong airport. There wasn't time to respond to all the messages. She decided to write Lilly and Oliver a quick note. It was brief and to the point: JUST B GLAD U GUYS GET 2 B 2GETHER. ALL ALONE & MISSING U, MILEY.

She pressed SEND. She knew she was

laying the guilt on thick as molasses. After all, with Roxy, her dad, and Jackson around, she wasn't *really* alone. But Miley figured her note would get the point across. She hated it when her friends fought. Especially when it was over lame stuff.

Miley hadn't wanted the flight attendants to see her without her wig so she wore a disguise to walk around the Hong Kong airport. That way, no one would spot Hannah. She had on a large coat, sunglasses, and a hat that hid most of her wig. She loaded up on souvenirs and bought some cool Chinese candy. When she and Roxy got back on the plane, Jackson and her father were already there.

Jackson had laid his beloved yellow surfboard on one of the leather benches. He knelt before it, lovingly polishing it with board butter and a rag.

Suddenly, it dawned on Miley: Jackson

was homesick! Just like she missed her friends, he missed Malibu. Miley felt a pang of sadness for her big brother. She had to break the weather news to him.

"Jackson, you realize that in Australia, it's—" A loud cough came from the other side of the plane. It was her dad interrupting her.

"Hey, bud, I need you for a second," he said. He looked at her pointedly and motioned for her to join him on the couch.

Miley went over. "Dad, don't you think we should tell him it's winter in Australia?" she whispered. "This seems cruel."

"But he's being so pleasant," said Mr. Stewart with a wry smile. "I hate to ruin his good mood. We'll tell him right before we get there."

Miley glanced at Jackson, who was happily whistling. Her dad had a point. Jackson *was* being pleasant. *Unusually* pleasant. He wasn't doing any of his typical annoying stuff, such as playing a really loud guitar game on the flat screen or forcing them to watch car chases.

"Okay," Miley conceded. "But he's really got his heart set on surfing. I think he misses Malibu. I feel sorry for him."

"He'll get over it as soon as we get there," said her dad. He glanced down at his Australia guidebook. The pages were tagged with Post-its in different colors. Mr. Stewart took sightseeing very seriously. "There's so much to do in Sydney. The museums, the harbor, the zoo. We can see kangaroos and koalas. Maybe catch a cricket match. And your brother can enjoy the beauty of Bondi Beach even if he can't surf there. You know, it's the most famous beach in the land Down Under."

"The land Down Under?" Miley repeated. It sounded vaguely familiar.

"Australia is in the lower half of the Southern Hemisphere," her dad explained. "The USA is in the Northern Hemisphere. So on a globe it seems like we live on top, and they live below. Get it? Down Under."

Miley thought about that for a second. Down Under. It made sense.

"Plus, you guys get to meet my old mate Hank Gibbons."

"Mate?" After Rome, Miley was psyched to be going to a country where they spoke English. Now it sounded like her dad was speaking a different language.

"In Australia, a mate means a good pal," Mr. Stewart explained.

"I didn't know you had a friend, I mean mate, in Australia," Miley said. "Lucky you." Miley wished she had a good friend in Sydney.

"Hank's an old buddy of mine. He's a talent manager. Haven't seen him in ages."

"Well, I can't wait to meet him, Daddy," Miley said. "I'm sure he's really nice."

"Nice? Not really," Mr. Stewart replied.

"Your friend—sorry, I mean your mate—isn't nice?" Miley was confused. Weren't the people you chose as friends supposed to be nice?

"Let's just say Hank can be competitive."

"About what?"

"Oh, anything. Cards, Ping-Pong, darts, Go Fish, who can snarf the most hot dogs in one sitting . . . ."

"*Ewwww!*" squealed Miley.

"You're telling me!? I won. Ate twenty-six of 'em. Buns included. Couldn't eat another dog for a decade. It wasn't until I started making my famous Hot Eee-Doggies for you and your brother that I started eating them again." Mr. Stewart winced at the disgusting memory. Still, Miley could hear the pride in his voice.

Miley felt queasy at the thought of eating twenty-six hot dogs. It was weird that her dad had done that to beat a friend. Apparently Oliver and Lilly weren't the only ones with friendship issues.

Miley thought about Amber and Ashley, the meanest, most popular girls in her grade. They were best friends—until one of them had something the other one wanted! Then their claws came out.

Miley's dad and his friend Hank sounded a little like Amber and Ashley. Only they were guys. And *really, really* old.

Miley didn't think it was possible. But midway through the flight from Hong Kong to Sydney, she fell asleep again. She woke up when the pilot announced: "We are now approaching Sydney, Australia. Please prepare for landing."

At long last—the words she'd been

waiting to hear! Miley didn't think she'd ever heard two sentences so beautiful in her entire life. Twenty-five hours! She'd made it.

Miley looked across the aisle. Her dad and Roxy were rubbing their eyes. They were just waking up, too. "Let's review Plans A, B, C, and Emergency Plan Z," ordered Roxy. Even though she was groggy, Roxy still managed to sound commanding and a little scary. She really was an excellent bodyguard.

As the plane began its descent, Miley and Roxy studied the maps of the airport. Roxy wanted Miley to understand all the possible routes they might take.

Then her wig needed adjustment after all of that sleeping. Hannah Montana couldn't meet the people of Sydney, Australia, for the first time with bed-wig!

Miley also needed a makeup touch-up. She had to be camera-ready in case any reporters were at the airport. That also meant she had to change out of her comfy traveling clothes. It was time for more glamorous Hannah apparel! Changing wasn't exactly easy. Especially because she was still wearing her seat belt!

By the time the plane finally landed, Miley was really excited. Not only were they in a new country and a new city—Australia was a whole different continent! It was the other side of the world. Boy, being an international superstar had its benefits.

In the flurry of activity, Miley had forgotten about Jackson and his surfing plans. The you-can-now-unbuckle-your-seat-belts sound dinged. Before Miley knew it, her brother had bounded out of his seat and raced down the aisle toward the exit. "Later, dudes, I mean, mates," he yelled happily. The worst part was he was wearing only a T-shirt, board shorts, and flip-flops. When had he changed out of his clothes?

Jackson ran full-steam ahead, clutching his shiny, waxed surfboard.

"*Jackson, no!!!!*" both Miley and Mr. Stewart screamed. But it was too late. Miley felt a gust of cold air as the plane doors opened and her brother stepped out.

Chapter Three

Jackson stepped onto the staircase that went down to the runway.

It was a bright July afternoon. The sky was a perfect bird's-egg blue. There wasn't a cloud to be seen. Waves, here I come! an ecstatic Jackson thought. And then a blast of cold air walloped him in the face.

Whaaaaat?

He held on to the railing to steady himself. It was chilly to the touch.

Jackson scurried down the stairs, using his

surfboard to protect him from the blustering winds. What was happening? All around him, airport workers were dressed in pants, jackets, and hats.

But it was July! Where was the summer weather?

Jackson was halfway down the staircase when his teeth started to chatter, and his legs started to tremble. It was too cold for shorts.

"*Ahhhhhhhhh!*" he screamed. He had to be quick. A crowd of reporters was just starting to approach the plane. He made a mad dash to the terminal. He had to get inside!

Shivering, Jackson wondered: why hadn't someone warned him?

Jackson wasn't the only one in for a shock. Miley stepped off the plane and was greeted by a blinding sea of flashing bulbs. Reporters and camera people were every-where: at the foot of the staircase, holding on to the railing, speeding past on luggage trolleys. "Hannah Montana," they all screamed.

"This way!"

"No, this way!"

"Over here!"

"No, over here!"

Ack! Miley knew Hannah Montana was popular in Australia. Still, she hadn't expected *this*. In Rome, there'd only been a few reporters. This was crazy. Full-scale crazy!

She smiled and waved as she walked steadily ahead, the wind whipping through her blond hair.

Airport security was in front of her, Roxy was in back. Miley felt Roxy's firm hand on her lower back. It pushed her forward. "Emergency Plan Z. That means just keep walking," Roxy directed. "No stopping. Look straight ahead. Don't look back. Just go, go, go!"

Miley tried to do what Roxy said. She

walked faster. But the reporters were so aggressive. "Just one shot, Miss Montana!" one pleaded, jumping right in front of her. He clicked his camera before he lost his balance and landed on the cold concrete. *Ouch!* That looked like it hurt!

"Are you okay?" Miley called to him. She didn't like the idea of anyone getting hurt.

"How 'bout just one more shot?" he called back.

"Fool," Miley heard Roxy mutter under her breath.

The most confusing part was all the reporters were barking questions at her about somebody named Gemma!

"Miss Montana, I need a comment about you and Gemma!" asked one.

"Yeah, what's your beef with our Gemma?" asked another.

"How does it feel to be in a celebrity

feud?" a different reporter asked.

A celebrity feud? Hannah Montana wasn't in a celebrity feud! And who was this Gemma?

Chapter Four

As soon as she got away from the crowd, Miley checked her phone for messages from Lilly and Oliver.

There was nothing. No texts or e-mails. Maybe it was the time difference. It's probably the middle of the night in Malibu, Miley figured.

Mr. Stewart and Jackson shared a car. Miley and Roxy took another one. Miley peered out the gray tinted windows of the limousine. A beautiful, unfamiliar city whizzed by. It was amazing how cities could be so different. Rome had been filled with old hilly streets, beautiful crumbling archways, and dark and mysterious crevices.

But Sydney was bright and open—new looking. The streets were broad, and everywhere Miley looked she saw water. It reminded her of driving on the Pacific Coast Highway that stretched from Malibu into northern California. She felt a sudden pang, wishing she could be at home.

"To your right," boomed the limo driver's voice over the speakers, "you'll see the magnificent Sydney Harbor, and the Sydney Opera House. I understand that's where you'll be performing, Miss Montana. At least that's what my excited daughters tell me."

"I've never performed at an opera house before," said Miley. "It's quite an honor." And she really meant it. The opera house was a modern white building that appeared to be rising from the glimmering turquoise water of Sydney Harbor. Wow, thought Miley, actually gulping for breath. The building was exquisite. And to think she'd be performing there! Sometimes Miley couldn't believe her life.

"Sydney is Australia's capital," the limo driver announced proudly. "When it's warm, people flock to our amazing beaches. I'm sure you've heard of Bondi Beach. It's famous for its waves."

Miley thought about Jackson in the other car. Her poor brother. His teeth had still been chattering when she left him. Miley hoped he was okay.

Miley tried to listen carefully as the driver told them about Sydney. But she kept getting distracted. The back of the limo was full of magazines. And Hannah Montana was on every cover!

HANNAH MONTANA VS. G'DAY, GEMMA!

read one cover. THE BATTLE OF THE TEEN STARS. LOCAL FAVORITE GEMMA VS. AMERICAN SUPERSTAR HANNAH MONTANA. WHO WILL WIN? read another. G'DAY, HANNAH. GEMMA'S GONNA SHOW YOU WHO'S THE TEEN QUEEN!

Finally Miley couldn't contain herself. She hadn't intended to be rude, but she interrupted the driver's lecture on the important bridges of Sydney to exclaim. "Who in the world is Gemma?"

The driver didn't seem to mind being interrupted. In fact, he seemed to like being asked a question. "She's the most popular chat-show host in Sydney, Miss Montana. About sixteen years old. My girls love her."

"Chat show?" Miley asked.

"A chat show in Australia is what we call a talk show," Roxy translated.

Boy, they sure said things differently in Australia.

"You can see for yourself," the driver told

Miley. "Her show's about to start." He pushed a button, and the television in the backseat came on. Miley stared as an image came into focus. It looked like a typical talk-show set—but with some teenage touches. The couch was soft and covered with neon throw pillows. There were posters on the wall. An announcer boomed: "She's Sydney's high school sweetheart. And she's here to school us all. Say g'day to . . . Gemma!"

A perky girl with curly brown hair ran onto the stage. She wore jeans, sneakers, and a hoodie. It was a lot like Miley's airplane outfit. The crowd cheered. Miley could hear some guys in the audience scream, "We love you, Gemma!"

"I love you, too!" Gemma yelled back. "And g'day, Sydney. What's up in our awesome city today?" More cheering from the crowd. Gemma rubbed her hands together and made a *brrrrr* sound. "Cold today, isn't

29

it? Hope our LA princess realizes that here it's winter in July."

Miley had the sinking feeling Gemma was talking about her.

"Then again, you know how isolated those Hollywood superstars can be. They think the sun follows them wherever they go." Gemma flounced around the set. Miley had the feeling she was making fun of one of Hannah Montana's dance moves. The crowd chuckled. "As of today, it's been ten days since my invitation. And no word back! She should name her next album *Rude*. What do you think of that?" Miley squirmed uncomfortably in her seat as the crowd cheered.

"Rude!? Sheesh," said Miley uneasily. "Why does she hate me so much?"

The limo driver answered. "According to Gemma, Hannah Montana—I mean, you— refused to come on Gemma's show. Didn't even respond to her invitation. But now that

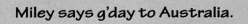

Miley says g'day to Australia.

Oliver hits the land Down Under.

Hannah's all set for the Sydney Opera House.

Lola loves being Hannah's best mate!

I've met you and see what a nice girl you are, I know that's not possible."

"Thanks," said Miley, feeling disturbed. The limo driver was right: it wasn't possible! Mr. Stewart was Hannah Montana's manager. It was his firm policy to respond to each and every request. Something was fishy about Gemma's story.

The driver pulled up to a large red-brick building with a gold awning. Miley didn't think she'd ever seen a building so long. It practically took up an entire city block! "We're here," he said. "The Sydney Hotel. The finest in luxury. Enjoy your time Down Under."

"I'm sure I will," said Miley. Then, just to further prove she wasn't as awful as Gemma said, she asked the driver if he'd like a signed CD to give his daughters. She always kept extras on hand.

A doorman whisked Miley into the

gleaming marble lobby. Once she was inside, she put aside all thoughts of Gemma. Now all she wanted to think about was a hot shower and a change of clothes. Twenty-five hours on an airplane meant twenty-five hours without a shower. It also meant twenty-five hours in the same socks and underwear. . . .

EWWWWWWWWW!

Chapter Five

What a difference a good shower
made!

Miley swished her just-dried, long brown
hair from side to side as she stepped out of
the bathroom. The suite filled with the scent
of lemon-verbena shampoo and conditioner.
Mmmmmmmm!

Miley loved checking out the fancy bath
products when she got to a hotel. This
time there had been a tiny bottle of peppermint foot scrub. Inside her boots, underneath

her socks, Miley could feel her refreshed toes tingling happily.

Miley was going to spend the day as herself, not Hannah Montana. She spotted Roxy, her dad, and Jackson in the hotel lobby. "Hey, guys!" she said. "I mean, g'day, mates."

They were meeting Mr. Stewart's old mate Hank Gibbons and his daughter at the Taronga Park Zoo. They hailed a taxi, then transferred to a tram and a ferry.

"You know, Hank's daughter is about your age," Mr. Stewart said as they stepped off the ferry. Cold air rose from the jetty. "Maybe you'll have an Aussie mate, too."

Miley rubbed her mittened hands together to keep warm. "Sure," she said. She didn't sound very enthusiastic. It wasn't that Miley wouldn't like having a new Australian friend, er, mate. But right now she was more concerned about her old friends.

Miley *still* hadn't heard from Lilly and

Oliver. She checked her cell phone every two minutes. Nothing. She was getting worried. Maybe they hadn't liked the message she sent. Maybe they didn't like being told to get along. Maybe they were mad at her.

She wavered back and forth. Could they be? Nah, they couldn't be. But maybe they were!

Ack! Not hearing from them was making Miley's mind play tricks on her.

"I can't wait to see me some koalas," said Roxy. "They're cute and cuddly on the outside. But they're fierce and ferocious on the inside. Like me!"

"I want to see a kangaroo," Mr. Stewart announced. "I've never seen one in person. The guidebook says there are more than fifty kinds of kangaroos."

"Wallabies sound cute to me," said Miley. "Plus they can jump up to six feet high." She'd read about them in the hotel guidebook.

Finally, they were inside the gates. "First stop, zoo café," Mr. Stewart announced. That's where they were meeting Mr. Gibbons and his daughter. That was fine with Miley. It suddenly dawned on her: she was starving!

"I think I'll catch up with the koalas," said Roxy. "Call me if you need me."

They might be on the other side of the world, but the zoo café had a very familiar menu. It was exactly like Rico's Surf Shop in Malibu. "*Mmm*, fries," said Miley, drinking in the delicious scent.

"Chips," said her father.

"I'm an American teenager. I know a french fry when I smell one!" Miley countered.

"What I mean is that in Australia they call fries *chips*."

That was the craziest thing Miley had ever heard. "Then what do they call *chips*?"

"Crisps," said Mr. Stewart.

Again Miley wondered how she'd be able to keep all this Aussie lingo straight.

A couple of rhinoceros-type snuffles came from behind her. Did they let animals into the café? Miley turned around nervously. Then she realized it was Jackson. His case of the shivers had turned into a full-blown cold. His eyes shone glassily. The tip of his nose looked swollen and red. "Ah cahn't snell a fing," he mumbled, shaking his head.

"What'd you say?" Miley asked.

"Ah cahn't snell a fing," he repeated woefully.

"What's that, son? Snails can't sing?" Mr. Stewart said.

Jackson sighed and tried pantomiming. But that just made it look as though he thought the zoo smelled. Finally he gave up.

Mr. Stewart patted him on the shoulder. "Don't worry. I'm sure it will smell just fine here." Then he spotted his friend. "Look, there's Hank!" he said, pointing to a table in the back. He waved. "Come on, kids, can't wait for you to meet my old mate!"

Like Mr. Stewart, Mr. Gibbons had tanned skin and longish hair. "You must be Miley," said Mr. Gibbons, holding out his hand. "A pleasure to meet you. And is that Jackson?"

Jackson sneezed.

There was an empty seat next to Miley's. "That's where my daughter is sitting. She just went to the WC," Hank explained. "She'll be back any second."

"WC?" Miley was confused.

"Water closet, it's what Australians call a bathroom," Mr. Stewart told her.

A water closet? Miley thought. That didn't even make any sense.

"I bet you and Gemma have a ton in common," said Mr. Gibbons. "You can find out for yourself—here she comes."

Gemma must be a popular name in Australia, thought Miley.

Miley turned to see a girl coming toward her. She weaved around the tables, smiling and waving. She had long curly hair and a perky walk. She looked a lot like the girl Miley had seen on TV earlier.

But it couldn't be.

That'd be too big a coincidence.

It'd be too weird. More than weird! Spooky, even.

The girl got a little closer.

Same bright blue eyes, same long lashes. Same dimpled smile, same freckled cheeks. And then Miley remembered Mr. Stewart saying that Mr. Gibbons was also a talent manager.

It was all coming together: her dad's friend's daughter was the bad-mouthing, celebrity-feuding Gemma from the chat show! The Gemma who hated Miley's—well, Hannah Montana's—guts.

What was Miley going to do now? Pretend this girl hadn't totally hurt her feelings? Act like everything was okay?

It seemed crazy, but that's what she had to do. Because Miley was Miley right now. She wasn't Hannah Montana. But she'd never wanted to spill the Hannah Montana beans more!

Miley took what her choreographer called a "deep yoga breath" to calm herself. Gemma approached.

"So you're Miley!" Gemma said with a sweet smile. "Wow! I'm so psyched to finally meet you."

Miley gave herself a silent pep talk in her head. It went: *be fake, be fake, be fake. You can do it. You know you can!*

She turned to Gemma, and in her friendliest voice, cooed: "Hi! It is *sooooooo* nice to meet you, too." She smiled a bright I'm-in-a-commercial-for-toothpaste smile.

"Wow," said Gemma. "I heard California girls were always happy. I guess it's really true."

Miley realized she was still smiling. Oops, she'd been concentrating so hard on being fake, she'd forgotten to move her face. She let her mouth go slack. How was she ever going to make it through this lunch?

Chapter Six

After a lunch filled with stories and Jackson's sniffles, it was time to walk around the zoo. Jackson was feeling so miserable he decided to stay in the café and have a mug of cocoa.

"Let's check out the wallabies," Gemma said as they left the café. "They're so cute. Like pint-size kangaroos—only nicer and furrier."

Of course, that was exactly what Miley wanted to do. Still, it annoyed her that

Gemma had suggested it first. Miley tried to stick close to her dad.

Except being with her dad right now was awful, too! He and Mr. Gibbons were still talking about all their old contests.

"No way, I'm the one who trounced *you* in Crazy Eights!" Mr. Stewart argued.

"Yeah, but I wiped the floor with you when we played Spit," shot back Mr. Gibbons.

They passed the baboon cages. One of the baboons was shoving a banana in another baboon's ear. Funny, they reminded Miley of her dad and Mr. Gibbons.

Miley heard a voice in her ear. "I can't listen to this another second." It was Gemma. Miley cringed. She'd been trying to avoid getting caught in a one-on-one conversation with Gemma. Now she had no choice. "Seems like our dads have a competitive friendship," said Gemma. "Those are the worst. Don't you think?"

"Yeah," said Miley, surprised. She hadn't been expecting Gemma to say something she agreed with.

Just then, Miley's cell phone chirped. "Sorry, just need to check something," she said. She reached into her coat pocket for her phone.

Two new messages! Finally, Oliver and Lilly had replied. Excitedly, Miley clicked open her in-box. Her heart sank. The messages were from Roxy. She'd sent Miley pictures of the koalas.

"Waiting to hear from someone important?" Gemma asked.

"Two people, actually," answered Miley. "My best friends."

"Lucky you," said Gemma. "I don't have best friends. I mean, I have friends, but not good ones. Basically, I'm working all the time."

"Right," said Miley, gritting her teeth. "I hear you're a really big star here."

"Kind of," Gemma said. "I've been getting more famous lately. There's this drama with the pop star Hannah Montana. You've heard of her, right?"

Miley nodded. A gust of wind blew past, and she pulled her scarf over her mouth. It helped to hide her smile.

"Dad called all the magazines when Hannah Montana refused to come on my show," Gemma explained.

"Refused?" Miley asked coyly. "She really refused? That doesn't sound like Hannah Montana."

"You know her?" Gemma asked.

"No, no, I've just read a lot about her," Miley said, stumbling. "She's supposed to be really nice."

"Well maybe, but she didn't respond to our request," said Gemma. "At least that's what Dad says. When the magazines found out, they put me on the cover. Hannah

Montana is big news. And the show's writers have been having me make all these mean jokes about her. Dad says Hannah Montana sells."

Nearby, a toddler was screaming for ice cream. The monkeys were making *eep-eep* noises. In the distance Miley could hear her dad and Mr. Gibbons fighting over who'd won at Ping-Pong. A thought entered Miley's head: maybe Gemma's father had made up the whole Hannah Montana invitation so his daughter would appear in more magazines. And poor Gemma had no idea!

"Look! We're here!" Gemma said, stopping short at a fenced-in grassy area. She pointed at two gray fuzz balls hopping around a tree stump. "Look! There are the wallabies! Aren't they the cutest things you've ever seen? I wish I could take one home with me."

"You'd definitely have the most original pet," Miley said.

"Yeah," Gemma agreed. "Also, I could use the company."

An unexpected feeling rose up in Miley. She felt a little sorry for Gemma. The poor girl seemed really lonely!

"Hey, girls." Mr. Gibbons and Mr. Stewart had finally caught up with them. "Miley," said Mr. Gibbons, "did Gemma tell you about her feud with your country's biggest pop star? Princess Hannah Montana?"

"Dad . . ." Gemma groaned.

"Well, Robby and I have been reminiscing about all the games we used to play. It gave me a brilliant idea. We should challenge Hannah Montana to compete against you at something! Something she's sure to lose in. Something really Australian. I know, boomerang!"

Boom-a-*whaat*? thought Miley.

"But Dad," Gemma said, "I thought she didn't even respond to our first invite."

47

"Robby here says she's staying at their hotel, and he can get the invite to her. He says he knows someone who knows her manager. He's sure she'll come."

Miley gave her dad a glare. Had he lost his mind? He wanted to beat Mr. Gibbons so badly he had agreed to a boomerang contest?! Miley had never even picked up a boomerang.

"But Dad," said Gemma, "Hannah Montana probably doesn't even know how to throw one."

"You can bet your sweet furry wallabies she doesn't," said Miley under her breath. Only Mr. Stewart heard her. He shot her a look.

"That's the point!" Mr. Gibbons boasted. "You'll make a mockery of her! Just like I made a mockery of Robby at backgammon back in—"

"Hey, I won that tournament," interrupted Mr. Stewart.

"Just imagine how many more magazines we'd get into," Mr. Gibbons said, rubbing his hands together menacingly, "once you crush Hannah Montana!"

"But, Dad . . ." Gemma looked like she might cry now. Miley's heart went out to her. "I don't want to make her look like a fool. Besides, haven't we gotten enough publicity from Hannah Montana?"

"Enough publicity!?" Mr. Gibbons scoffed. "No such thing!"

It looked like Gemma and her dad were going to be arguing for a while. So Mr. Stewart said they had to go. "We've got some friends meeting us back at the hotel," he told them.

"We do?" Miley asked. "Who?"

"You'll see," he said mysteriously. "Now let's collect your brother at the café and go."

Chapter Seven

"**L**illy!" Miley yelled when she opened the door to her room.

Miley's best friend in the world was sitting on the sofa. She wore a fluffy white hotel robe. Her long blond hair was up in a towel, turban-style.

"*Eeep!* My Miley!" Lilly shouted happily, wiggling her feet. "Have you tried this peppermint foot lotion? It's amazing!" Miley laughed. Of course Lilly had gone straight for the bath products.

"So you're not mad at me?" Miley asked. She hugged her friend.

"Why would I be mad at you?" Lilly asked.

"I thought maybe you didn't like the message I sent you. About how you and Oliver should get along."

"No way!" said Lilly. "I loved it. You were totally right. Oliver and I needed to stop arguing. We were being babies. Plus, it was perfect timing! We got your message right before we got on the flight."

"We?" Miley was confused.

"Yeah, Oliver's here, too. We were on a flight for twenty-five hours together and we never fought once. Thanks to you! He's staying in Jackson's room. So what's the haps here?"

Boy, did Miley have a lot to tell Lilly! "Oh, gosh," she said, bouncing onto the sofa. "I barely know where to start. But first let me ask you this. Have you ever heard of a boomerang?"

Oliver's mom had a thing about germs. She hated them. She'd loaded Oliver's suitcases with tubes and tubes of antibacterial hand gel. Good thing, too! After thirty seconds in Jackson's room, Oliver felt like he needed to take a bath in the stuff.

"I'mb tick," Jackson had told Oliver when he answered the door.

"You're thick? Yeah, well maybe a little," Oliver agreed good-naturedly.

"No, I'mb tick," Jackson repeated.

"You're . . . ?" Oliver still couldn't make out that second word.

Then Jackson sneezed a massive, gross, gooey sneeze, spraying germs every which way. "Dude!" Oliver screeched. "Oh, I get it! You're sick."

He made a beeline for the lobby. He'd

have to ask for another room. No way was he staying with Jackson, aka Germson!

Oliver called Miley and Lilly and went up to say hi. Miley had been thrilled. But then she and Lilly started talking about boomerangs and peppermint foot lotion. So Oliver decided to see about getting a new room.

The lobby of the Sydney Hotel was a very nice place: plush sofas to sit on, magazines to read, little bowls of nuts to nibble on. The guy behind the desk kept saying a room would open up soon. But Oliver had been waiting for an hour.

He was slumped on a sofa, feeling sorry for himself when he heard a girl asking for Miley.

"Hi, I was wondering if a Miley Stewart is staying here?" the girl asked the man at the front desk. The girl had brown curly hair half-hidden under a baseball cap, and an Australian accent. "I've been trying to get in touch with her."

Oliver knew that Miley used fake names when she checked into hotels. So he jumped up and interrupted.

"Hey! I'm a friend of Miley's. Can I help you with something?"

"Oh," said the girl, smiling. "I was wondering if she wanted to go out to dinner with me. She and I hung out with our dads today. I thought maybe she could use some girl time. I know I could."

Girl time! thought Oliver, that's what Miley and Lilly are doing. He couldn't see much of this girl's face. She was wearing sunglasses. But what he could see was awfully cute. Then he had an idea.

"I think Miley was going to sleep," he said. "Anyway, girl time is overrated, don't you think?"

"Not really," said Gemma with a giggle.

Oliver wasn't usually bold. But he couldn't stand the hotel lobby. So far, his trip to

Sydney was a bomb. But it'd be *the* bomb if he managed to get a date with an Australian hottie on the first night!

"You could pretend I was a girl," Oliver offered. He immediately realized how dumb that sounded.

"Excuse me?"

"I mean, you could have girl time with me." He wasn't making this any better. "I-I-I'm a guy, not a girl, but I c-c-could hang out with you," Oliver stammered.

He'd blown it. He was sure of it. But then, the most shocking thing happened. "I need a break," Gemma said. "I guess I won't get any girl time, but you seem nice. And if Miley's friends with you, that's good enough for me. You like hamburgers? And by the way," the girl said, "I'm Gemma. It's nice to meet you."

With that, Oliver bid the lobby of the Sydney Hotel a happy good-bye.

Chapter Eight

Jackson couldn't get comfortable. If he slept on his back, it made his nose feel clogged up. If he slept on his stomach, it made his nose run.

It was 3:15 in the morning and he had barely slept a wink. And why did the numbers on the clock have to be so bright? Jackson threw a pillow over the clock. He moaned. Now it was too dark.

Jackson tried to play a video game on the hotel TV. But his eyes were so tired and watery, the screen turned blurry. He tried to watch TV. There was an old surfing competition on the Australian sports channel. It just reminded him of how sick he was. And why.

Lame. This was so lame.

He decided maybe he was hungry. Maybe a full stomach would help him sleep. If they were at home his dad would make him chicken soup. Boy, he'd love some chicken soup now. Then he remembered he was in a hotel—that meant tasty treats 24/7.

It took several rings for someone to answer. "Hello, room service, how can I help you?" the voice asked.

Jackson started to talk, but no words came out. All that came from his mouth was a half-wheeze, half-cough. It sounded like this: "*Scraggggggg.*"

"I'm sorry, sir, couldn't hear you," said the voice.

"*Blurghh . . . scraggg . . . ka-blech,*" said Jackson, trying to clear his throat and get a word out.

"Okay, I think this is a bad connection. Thank you for your call."

"Shoot," said Jackson, though it sounded more like "*ploof.*"

He decided to drink a glass of water and try again. "Hello, room service, how can I help you?" the voice asked again.

"*Tum sicken zoop pleeth,*" Jackson said, trying to pronounce each word carefully.

There was a long pause. "I'm sorry, sir, could you repeat that?"

"*Tum sicken zoop pleeth,*" Jackson repeated with a sigh.

"I'm sorry, sir, could you repeat that?"

"*Sicken zoop!*" Jackson warbled.

"Liverwurst?" the room-service guy asked.

"*Sicken zoop!*" Jackson told him.

"A medley of fruit?"

"*Sicken zoop!*" Jackson repeated. Why couldn't this guy understand that he wanted some chicken soup?

"Okay, liverwurst and a medley of fruit it is," said the voice.

"Oh, jussss fuhget it," Jackson grumbled hoarsely. He hung up the phone and turned off the light.

At 4:15a.m., Jackson had finally drifted off into an uneasy snooze. There was a knock at the door.

Jackson pulled the covers over his head.

Knock, knock.

He opened his eyes and blinked into the darkness. "Room service," called a voice. "Did somebody order liverwurst and a medley of fruit?"

Jackson groaned and put a pillow over his head.

Chapter Nine

"Come on—up, up, up!" shouted Lilly. She pulled the curtains and stood beside Miley's bed. "Let's get our boomerang on!"

"Ugh," Miley moaned, shielding her eyes from the bright light. "Lilly"—she groaned, turning over—"I'm having a hard time taking you seriously."

"Why? Because I just said 'Let's get our boomerang on?'"

"That, and your pajamas."

Lilly looked down. She was wearing her

favorite cupcake pajamas. "Oops," she said. "I should be wearing my sushi pajamas. They're healthier."

"I don't know how I'm supposed to win this contest—I've never even picked up a boomerang," Miley said. She covered her face with the comforter.

"No problem," Lilly said enthusiastically. "I've been doing some research." She bounced over to Miley's laptop and read aloud. "A boomerang is a flat, curved wooden tool used for sport. When hurled correctly, it returns to the thrower."

"Huh?" groaned Miley. "I've never hurled anything in my life."

"And look!" Lilly said, showing Miley a strange L-shaped object. "Your dad put one under the door while we were sleeping. This is your boomerang."

Miley held the wooden "hurling thing" in her hand, wishing she could go back to sleep.

* * *

$\mathscr{B}$ondi Beach! Miley had read about it in the guidebooks. It was one of Sydney's most popular beaches and where Jackson had planned to surf. It was flat and wide, and on this wintry morning, completely empty. It was the perfect place to practice hurling a boomerang.

"Move, Stewart, move!" shouted Roxy into a megaphone. Miley did jumping jacks. Sand flew every which way. "I don't care how cold it is! *Moooooooove*!"

Lilly did a cartwheel in the sand and cheered: "Gimme a B! Gimme an O! Gimme another O! Gimme an M! What does it spell? BOOM? Who puts the boom in boomerang? Miley that's whom!" She stopped moving. "I know it should be who, but *whom* rhymes with *boom*."

"I won't tell the grammar police," Miley said, panting. "Did you make that up on the fly?"

"Yup," said Lilly, jogging in place to keep warm.

"Not bad," said Miley. Once, a really long time ago, Miley and Lilly had tried out for the cheerleading squad. Lilly made it. Miley made mascot. It turned out Lilly really did have skills.

Speaking of skills . . . when it came to the boomerang, Miley didn't have many. She gripped the strange wooden object like a Frisbee and prepared to throw it. "Stop!" Lilly shouted. "You're supposed to throw it overhand, like a baseball."

"I don't know how to throw a baseball!" Miley shouted back. Though, as her best friend, of course Lilly already knew that.

"Here, let Roxy school you." Roxy came marching over and took the boomerang from Miley. "Hold the boomerang in your right hand. Bend your arm back so your hand is near your right ear. Then let go using as much force as you got." Then she hurled the boomerang.

Miley watched it fly through the air and circle back to Roxy. How did Roxy always know how to do things like this? she wondered.

Then Miley tried.

The boomerang dropped to the ground.

She tried again, raising it high above her ear and letting it go. It clocked her on the back of the head. "Ow!" she yelped.

"You okay?" asked Lilly.

Waves crashed. The crisp air howled. They kept going for another couple of hours. By the time they had to go, Miley could throw the boomerang. It even came back to her, sort of.

It probably wasn't good enough to win. But it was good enough to make sure she didn't look like an idiot.

Miley smiled at Roxy and Lilly gratefully. She was tired, cold, and winded. But she was ready.

Chapter Ten

$\mathcal{M}$iley and Lilly, dressed as Hannah Montana and her friend Lola Luftnagle, were in the elevator at the television studio where *G'Day, Gemma* was taped. "Got the boomerang?" Miley asked.

"Right here," said Lilly, taking it from her bag. "May the best boomeranger win."

"Actually," said Miley, "maybe you should hope for the opposite."

The first person Miley saw was the last person she expected to see: Oliver! He was sitting on the sofa in the lounge, sipping a soda.

"What are you doing here?" Miley whispered.

"Well, last night I met this girl. Really cute, named Gemma. She was at the hotel looking for you."

"For me as in Hannah Montana?" Miley whispered.

"Nope, she wanted to hang with Miley. But since you were occupied, she ended up hanging with me instead." Oliver puffed out his chest proudly. "The women of Australia can't resist my charms, I guess."

Oliver grinned smugly. Lilly rolled her eyes. Miley wagged her finger at them to behave. "Go on, go on," she told Oliver.

"We went out for burgers, and then we went to the Sydney Aquarium." He smiled at the memory. "We had a blast. When she dropped me back at the hotel, she asked me to meet her here this morning. I had no idea she was some big star." Oliver arched his eyebrows and lowered his voice, looking around to see that no one was listening. "Also, I had no idea you were in a celebrity feud with her."

"I'm not," Miley whispered. She looked around to see if anyone saw her. "It's not real. Her dad made it up. Forget it, it's too complicated to explain."

"You don't have to. I already figured that out. And that's what I told her."

"You told her?!?" Miley and Lilly shrieked at once. You could hear the panic in their voices. Had Oliver blown Hannah Montana's cover?

"Yeah, I told her that I had a friend who met Hannah Montana, and that there was no way she'd be a no-show. I said I didn't believe it. I said I'd once met her manager, too, and that he wouldn't ignore a request."

"And then what?"

"She said she didn't believe it either. She

was beginning to suspect it was a publicity stunt that her dad made up."

"So now where is she?" Miley asked.

"Having a massive fight with him in the dressing room," Oliver said. "They've been in there for an hour. But I don't think there's going to be a show today. I heard a producer say they're going to go with a rerun."

Miley felt bad. She didn't agree with what Mr. Gibbons had done, but he was Gemma's dad. It must be hard for Gemma if she couldn't trust him.

"So no contest?" Lilly asked, twirling the boomerang in her hand.

"Nope," said Oliver. "You're free."

"Wow, way to save the day," said Miley.

"Hey, what are friends for?" said Oliver, managing to sound both humble and proud at once.

"Sorry we needed girl time last night," Miley said.

"It's okay," said Oliver. "It all turned out for the best. When the hotel guy saw me hanging out with a big star like Gemma, he hooked me up with an awesome suite. You guys can come over for room service after the show if you want."

"Deal," said Miley.

"I can't believe no boomerang," said Lilly. She actually looked a little disappointed. "All our training."

"Lilly, that boomerang is my gift to you. You're such a good friend. You spent all that time training me. You put the 'boom' in boomerang."

"Awesome!" said Lilly. "I'm going to bring this home. Maybe do some boomerang-throwing on the beach. Maybe I can start a new trend!"

"So now what do we do?" Miley wondered. "I don't have to be at the sound check for two hours." For the first time since she'd

69

arrived in Sydney, she had some free time. "Shopping?" she asked Lilly and Oliver. "I've been dying to hit the streets. Maybe we could even go to a waterfront café, get some seafood."

"I'm in," said Lilly.

"Great," said Miley. "Let's change back into us. You coming, Oliver? Can you handle a little girl time?"

"Actually," he said, blushing, "I'm going to wait for Gemma. Can I meet you in an hour or so?"

"Sure. Tell her g'day from us!" Miley called.

Mr. Stewart was waiting for them in a limousine in front of the set. They told him what had happened. "I'm sorry I didn't get the chance to beat her at boomerang, Dad. I know it meant a lot to you."

"I'm sorry I ever asked you to try, bud," her dad said, shaking his head. "I can't believe

I got caught up in such a petty rivalry. I feel bad for the guy. He really stooped low. Just to get ahead. It's sad when you think about it."

A few minutes later, his cell phone buzzed. He had a text. "Speak of the devil," said Mr. Stewart.

"What is it?" Miley asked.

"It's Hank. He's challenged me to a game of Spit this afternoon."

"Ha!" said Lilly. "As if you'd go play a dumb game like Spit."

Miley looked at her dad. "You wouldn't do that, right, Dad?" She wasn't so sure.

"Hmmmm, well. Yeah, maybe I might," Mr. Stewart said. Miley and Lilly gaped. Did they hear what they just thought they heard? Mr. Stewart gave them a sheepish smile. "What can I say? The guy brings out the fighter in me. Hey, it's just a little harmless fun. Besides I have some time after sound check."

Miley and Lilly shook their heads in disbelief. "Competitive friendships are the worst," Lilly said.

Miley couldn't agree more. Then off they went to explore the amazing city of Sydney.

Chapter Eleven

*M*iley burst into the dressing room after her show. She couldn't believe she'd actually gotten to sing at the Sydney Opera House. She'd always thought it looked like a cool building from the outside. Her show had been in the concert hall. The acoustics were so amazing that she'd even done two songs a cappella.

The crowd had loved it. They seemed to know all of her songs, and she had two encores.

Lilly stuck her head into the dressing room.

She was wearing a bright red wig, part of her disguise as Hannah's friend Lola Luftnagle. "Looked great from backstage," she said.

Then Gemma and Oliver appeared.

"It's so nice to finally meet you," Gemma said. "I'm really sorry for all that business in the magazines. It turned out there was a big misunderstanding with the invitation. I'm sorry I fell for it."

Miley smiled at her. "It's okay. These things happen. I'm just glad you could come to the concert."

"Yes, thanks so much for the tickets. Oh, I want you to meet a friend of mine. This is Oliver, from America."

Miley shook Oliver's hand. "Pleased to meet you," she said, doing her best to keep a straight face. "What brings you to Australia?"

"Oh, I'm just here visiting my friend Miley," he replied.

"I bet you'd like her," Gemma told Hannah.

"Ya think?" Oliver said, with a quick grin at Miley.

"Of course. We should all go out for some chips," Gemma answered.

"I can't—I'm meeting some people after the show," Hannah said. "But thanks—and definitely look me up if you ever come to California."

Later that night, Miley, Lilly, and Oliver gathered in the hotel suite.

"What a night," Lilly said. "I can't believe everyone kept a straight face in the dressing room."

"It sure wasn't easy," Oliver said.

"Ya think?" Miley answered, shoving him playfully as they all burst into laughter.

Just then, Jackson and Mr. Stewart walked in. Mr. Stewart was carrying a covered tray.

"Where to next?" Jackson asked. He finally felt better.

"Brazil, son," said Mr. Stewart. "Tropical

climate, I'm happy to report. You're gonna need your surfboard."

Jackson grinned. It was all packed up and ready to go. And it was polished, too!

"It's back to Malibu for us," Lilly said, gesturing to Oliver.

"Before we go, I wanted to share a gift that Hank gave me to remember our time here." Mr. Stewart lifted the cover off the tray. It was stacked high with hot dogs.

Miley groaned. "How many this time, Daddy?"

"Twenty-seven, Mile. Hank's note said something about staying in shape for our next contest."

Miley groaned again. Then she dug in. They may not have been Hot Eee-Doggies, but it had been a long day and she was starving.

As everyone ate, Miley glanced over at the boomerang sticking out of Lilly's bag. One thing was for sure—she'd never forget the land Down Under.